Rocky Creek Elementary Library
Lexington, S.C.

MONSTERS

ILLUSTRATED BY
MARTIN ONTIVEROS

GROWLING IN THE BACKGROUND

Halloween Poems For The Brave

Reycraft Books
55 Fifth Avenue
New York, NY 10003

Reycraftbooks.com

Reycraft Books is a trade imprint and trademark of Newmark Learning, LLC.

"Halloween Party" from *When The Teacher Isn't Looking* by Kenn Nesbitt, copyright © 2010. Reprinted by permission of Running Press Kids, an imprint of Hachette Book Group, Inc. "The Ghost" courtesy Richard Jones. "Ghost Bus" courtesy of Pieces of Learning, Inc. "Skeleton Pranksters on Halloween Night" Courtesy of Kelly S. Roper. "Halloween" courtesy of Carole Kancar. "Mr. Macklin's Jack O'Lantern" from *Every Time I Climb a Tree* by David McCord, copyright © 1967. Reprinted by permission of Little, Brown, an imprint of Hachette Book Group, Inc.

All rights reserved. No portion of this book may be reproduced, stored in a retrieval system, or transmitted in any form or by any means, electronic, mechanical, photocopying, recording, or otherwise, without written permission from the publisher. For information regarding permission, please contact info@reycraftbooks.com.

Educators and Librarians: Our books may be purchased in bulk for promotional, educational, or business use. Please contact sales@reycraftbooks.com.

Sale of this book without a front cover or jacket may be unauthorized. If this book is coverless, it may have been reported to the publisher as "unsold or destroyed" and may have deprived the author and publisher of payment.

Library of Congress Control Number: 2022903853

ISBN: 978-1-4788-7041-8

Printed in Dongguan, China. 8557/0522/19057

10 9 8 7 6 5 4 3 2 1

Illustrator photo courtesy of Martin Ontiveros

First Edition Hardcover published by Reycraft Books 2022.

Reycraft Books and Newmark Learning, LLC, support diversity and the First Amendment, and celebrate the right to read.

It was a dark and stormy night, as all good Halloween nights should be. My friends and I threw on our costumes, ready for candy and some creepy fun. One was a superhero. Another a clown. The last a famous movie villain and I dressed as a pickle.

As we crossed the street in front of the cemetery, we noticed dark figures rising from the graves. Then strange shapes appeared on the dimly lit sidewalk in front of us. The sounds—distant, unfamiliar, and growing louder—were the sounds of monsters growling in the background. We turned to run, but as we did a creature with dripping, red fangs blocked our way. I let out a shriek that started deep in my gut and exploded into the darkness. A tingling, like a thousand tiny spiders, moved up and down my spine and shot out of my legs as I fell to the ground.

That's the last thing I remember about that night.

I have collected these poems—some as old as a rotting corpse in a grave, others as new as a baby goblin—to capture what we felt that night. I suggest you read them with the lights on or . . . just maybe . . . with them off. But only if you dare!

Halloween Party
by Kenn Nesbitt

We're having a Halloween party at school.
I'm dressed up like Dracula. Man, I look cool!
I dyed my hair black, and I cut off my bangs.
I'm wearing a cape and some fake plastic fangs.

I put on some makeup to paint my face white,
like creatures that only come out in the night.
My fingernails, too, are all pointed and red.
I look like I'm recently back from the dead.

My mom drops me off, and I run into school
and suddenly feel like the world's biggest fool.
The other kids stare like I'm some kind of freak—
the Halloween party is not till next week.

THE NIGHT WIND
by Eugene Field

Have you ever heard the wind go "Yooooo"?
'Tis a pitiful sound to hear!
It seems to chill you through and through
With a strange and speechless fear.
'Tis the voice of the night that broods outside
When folk should be asleep,
And many and many's the time I've cried
To the darkness brooding far and wide
Over the land and the deep:
"Whom do you want, O lonely night,
That you wail the long hours through?"
And the night would say in its ghostly way:

"YOOOOOOOO! YOOOOOOOO! YOOOOOOOO!"

My mother told me long ago
(When I was a little tad)
That when the night went wailing so,
   Somebody had been bad;
And then, when I was snug in bed,
   Whither I had been sent,
With the blankets pulled up round my head,
I'd think of what my mother'd said,
And wonder what boy she meant!
And "Who's been bad today?"
I'd ask, Of the wind that hoarsely blew,
And the voice would say in its meaningful way:

"YOOOOOOOO! YOOOOOOOO! YOOOOOOOOO!"

That this was true I must allow—
You'll not believe it, though!
Yes, though I'm quite a model now,
I was not always so.
And if you doubt what things I say,
Suppose you make the test;
Suppose, when you've been bad some day
And up to bed are sent away
From mother and the rest—
Suppose you ask, "Who has been bad?"
And then you'll hear what's true;
For the wind will moan in its ruefullest tone:

"YOOOOOOOO! YOOOOOOOO!
"YOOOOOOOO!"

The Ghost
by Richard Jones

I live in a house with no windows
a black curtain hangs on my door.
The voices of conscience torment me
I live in a room with no floor.
There's dirt in the corner I can't see
there's water that runs down the wall.
There're mice in the attic above me
and rats playing games in the hall.
I live in a house with no windows
and sleep in a room with no heat.
The darkness of life that surrounds me
keeps out the sounds of the street.
I wake when the shadows have fallen
and walk when the memories cease.
When purpose in life has no meaning
and only the wicked find peace.
Each night you sense that I'm by you
you feel my breath as you sleep.
You hear the faint creak of the floorboards
as out from the shadows I creep.
I live in a house with no windows
I live in a house that's now yours
It's my voice you think that you're hearing
for I died in this room with no doors.

Song of the Witches:
"Double, double toil and trouble"
by William Shakespeare
(from Macbeth IV.i 10-19; 35-38)

Double, double toil and trouble;
Fire burn and caldron bubble.
Fillet of a fenny snake,
In the caldron boil and bake;
Eye of newt and toe of frog,
Wool of bat and tongue of dog,
Adder's fork and blind-worm's sting,
Lizard's leg and howlet's wing,
For a charm of powerful trouble,
Like a hell-broth boil and bubble.

Double, double toil and trouble;
Fire burn and caldron bubble.
Cool it with a baboon's blood,
Then the charm is firm and good.

THE LITTLE GHOST
by Edna St. Vincent Millay

I knew her for a little ghost
    That in my garden walked;
The wall is high—higher than most—
    And the green gate was locked.
And yet I did not think of that
    Till after she was gone—
I knew her by the broad white hat,
    All ruffled, she had on.
By the dear ruffles round her feet,
    By her small hands that hung
In their lace mitts, austere and sweet,
    Her gown's white folds among.
I watched to see if she would stay,
    What she would do—and oh!
She looked as if she liked the way
    I let my garden grow!
She bent above my favorite mint
    With conscious garden grace,
She smiled and smiled—there was no hint
    Of sadness in her face.
She held her gown on either side
    To let her slippers show,
And up the walk she went with pride,
    The way great ladies go.
And where the wall is built in new
    And is of ivy bare
She paused—then opened and passed through
    A gate that once was there.

The Spider and The Fly: A Fable
by Mary Howitt

"Will you walk into my parlor?" said a spider to a fly;
"'Tis the prettiest little parlor that ever you did spy.
The way into my parlor is up a winding stair,
And I have many pretty things to show when you are there."
"Oh no, no!" said the little fly, "to ask me is in vain,
For who goes up your winding stair can ne'er come down again."

"I'm sure you must be weary, with soaring up so high,
Will you rest upon my little bed?" said the spider to the fly.
"There are pretty curtains drawn around, the sheets are fine and thin;
And if you like to rest awhile, I'll snugly tuck you in."
"Oh no, no!" said the little fly, "for I've often heard it said,
They never, never wake again, who sleep upon your bed!"

Said the cunning spider to the fly, "Dear friend, what shall I do,
To prove the warm affection I've always felt for you?
I have, within my pantry, good store of all that's nice;
I'm sure you're very welcome—will you please to take a slice?"

"Oh no, no!" said the little fly, "kind sir, that cannot be,
I've heard what's in your pantry, and I do not wish to see."

"Sweet creature!" said the spider, "you're witty and you're wise.
How handsome are your gauzy wings, how brilliant are your eyes!
I have a little looking-glass upon my parlor shelf,
If you'll step in one moment, dear, you shall behold yourself."
"I thank you, gentle sir," she said, "for what you're pleased to say,
And bidding you good morning now, I'll call another day."

The spider turned him round about, and went into his den,
For well he knew, the silly fly would soon come back again:
So he wove a subtle web, in a little corner, sly,
And set his table ready, to dine upon the fly.
Then he went out to his door again, and merrily did sing,
"Come hither, hither, pretty fly, with the pearl and silver wing;
Your robes are green and purple—there's a crest upon your head;
Your eyes are like the diamond bright, but mine are dull as lead."

Alas, alas! how very soon this silly little fly,
Hearing his wily, flattering words, came slowly flitting by;
With buzzing wings she hung aloft, then near and nearer drew,
Thinking only of her brilliant eyes, and green and purple hue—
Thinking only of her crested head, poor foolish thing!—At last
Up jumped the cunning spider, and fiercely held her fast.

He dragged her up his winding stair, into his dismal den,
Within his little parlor—but she ne'er came out again!
—And now, dear little children, who may this story read,
To idle, silly, flattering words, I pray you ne'er give heed:
Unto an evil counsellor, close heart, and ear, and eye,
And take a lesson from this tale, of the Spider and the Fly.

Skeleton Pranksters on Halloween Night
by Kelly Roper

Halloween night is the special time
Little skeletons come out to play.
They frolic in the merry moonlight,
And many pranks they play.

They love to hide in the bushes,
And rustle them as children pass by.
They like to lurk in the shadows,
And surprise with a disembodied sigh.

They sometimes like to tag along
Behind innocent trick-or-treaters,
Only to reveal their true bony selves,
And turn kids into little beat-feeters.

And they're not above snatching candy
Right out of unfortunate kids' bags.
That's one of their favorite tricks to play,
These skinless, little scallywags.

So beware, you masked junior witches
And pretend little ghosts and ghouls.
These little skeletons can be devilish,
And they'd love to play a trick on you!

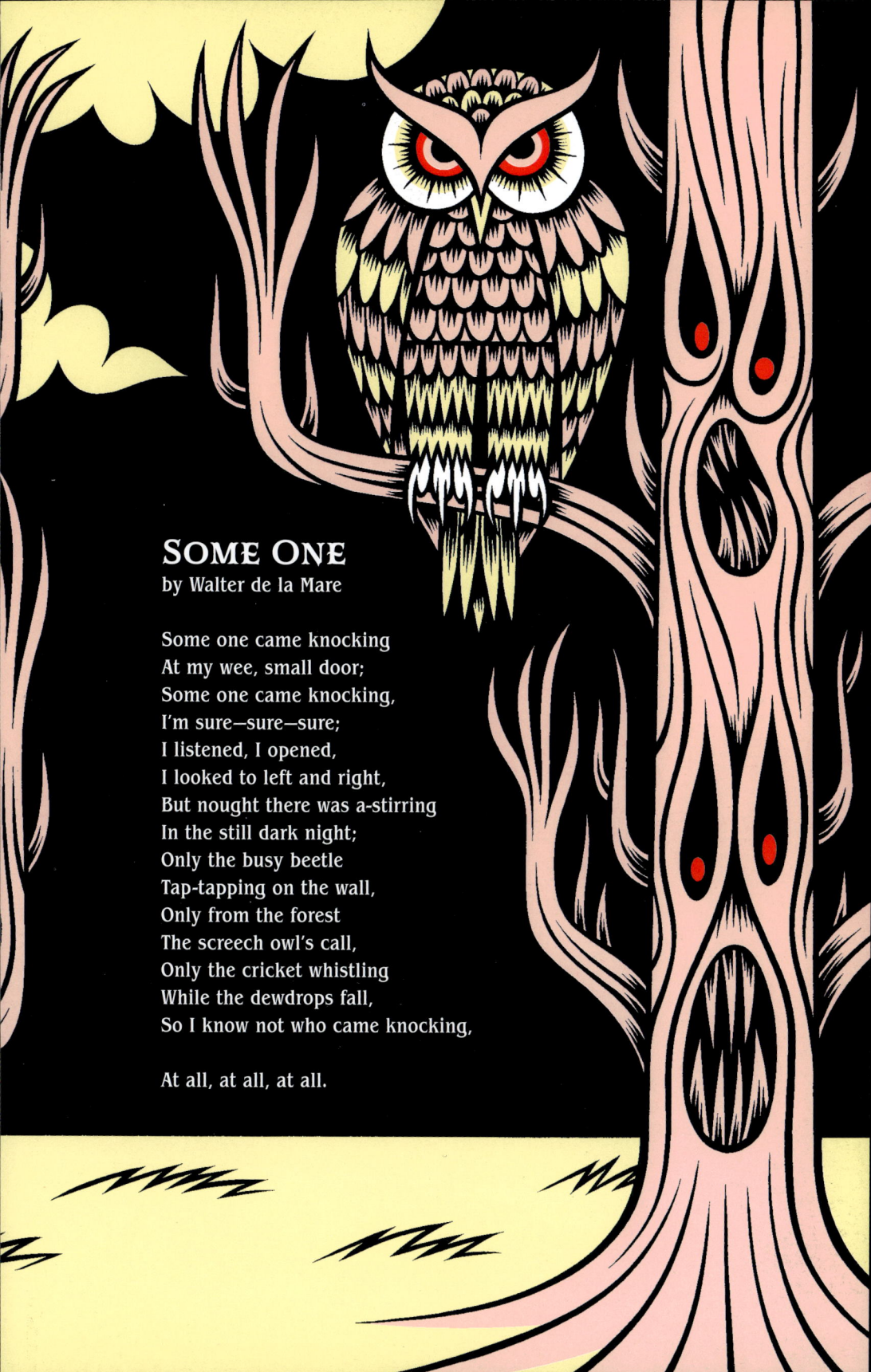

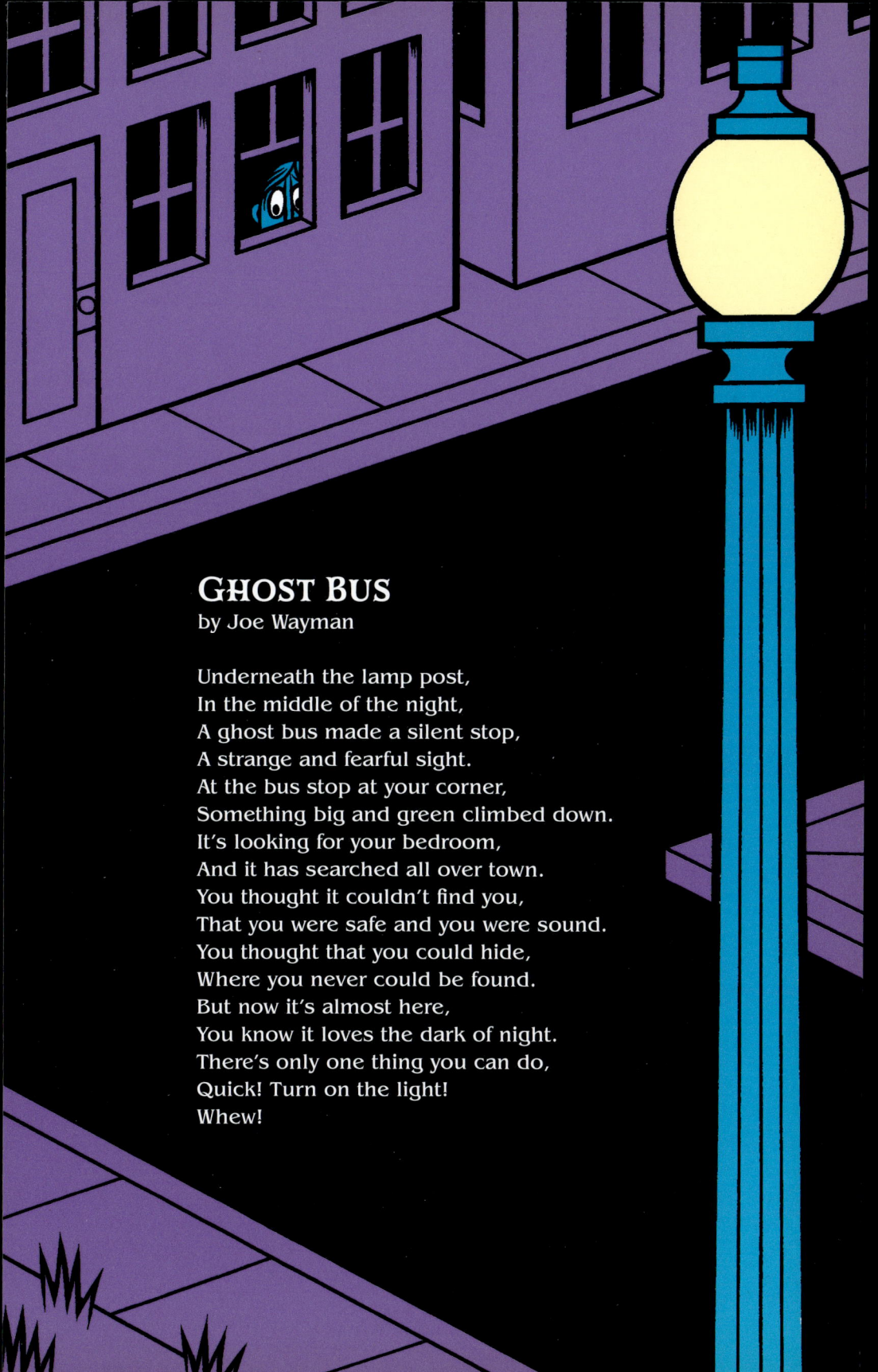

GHOST BUS
by Joe Wayman

Underneath the lamp post,
In the middle of the night,
A ghost bus made a silent stop,
A strange and fearful sight.
At the bus stop at your corner,
Something big and green climbed down.
It's looking for your bedroom,
And it has searched all over town.
You thought it couldn't find you,
That you were safe and you were sound.
You thought that you could hide,
Where you never could be found.
But now it's almost here,
You know it loves the dark of night.
There's only one thing you can do,
Quick! Turn on the light!
Whew!

MR. MACKLIN'S JACK O'LANTERN
by David McCord

Mr. Macklin takes his knife
And carves the yellow pumpkin face:
Three holes bring eyes and nose to life,
The mouth has thirteen teeth in place.
Then Mr. Macklin just for fun
Transfers the corn-cob pipe from his
Wry mouth to Jack's, and everyone
Dies laughing! O what fun it is
Till Mr. Macklin draws the shade
And lights the candle in Jack's skull.
Then all the inside dark is made
As spooky and as horrorful
As Halloween, and creepy crawl
The shadows on the tool-house floor,
With Jack's face dancing on the wall.
O Mr. Macklin! Where's the door?

THE RAVEN
by Edgar Allan Poe

Once upon a midnight dreary, while I pondered, weak and weary,
Over many a quaint and curious volume of forgotten lore—
    While I nodded, nearly napping, suddenly there came a tapping,
As of some one gently rapping, rapping at my chamber door.
"'Tis some visitor," I muttered, "tapping at my chamber door—
        Only this and nothing more."

    Ah, distinctly I remember it was in the bleak December;
And each separate dying ember wrought its ghost upon the floor.
    Eagerly I wished the morrow;—vainly I had sought to borrow
    From my books surcease of sorrow—sorrow for the lost Lenore—
For the rare and radiant maiden whom the angels name Lenore—
        Nameless here for evermore.

    And the silken, sad, uncertain rustling of each purple curtain
Thrilled me—filled me with fantastic terrors never felt before;
    So that now, to still the beating of my heart, I stood repeating
    "'Tis some visitor entreating entrance at my chamber door—

Continued...

Some late visitor entreating entrance at my chamber door;—
      This it is and nothing more."

  Presently my soul grew stronger; hesitating then no longer,
"Sir," said I, "or Madam, truly your forgiveness I implore;
  But the fact is I was napping, and so gently you came rapping,
  And so faintly you came tapping, tapping at my chamber door,
That I scarce was sure I heard you"—here I opened wide the door;—
      Darkness there and nothing more.

  Deep into that darkness peering, long I stood there wondering, fearing,
Doubting, dreaming dreams no mortal ever dared to dream before;
  But the silence was unbroken, and the stillness gave no token,
  And the only word there spoken was the whispered word, "Lenore?"

This I whispered, and an echo murmured back the word, "Lenore!"—
      Merely this and nothing more.

  Back into the chamber turning, all my soul within me burning,
Soon again I heard a tapping somewhat louder than before.
  "Surely," said I, "surely that is something at my window lattice;
  Let me see, then, what thereat is, and this mystery explore—
Let my heart be still a moment and this mystery explore;—
      'Tis the wind and nothing more!"

    Open here I flung the shutter, when, with many a flirt and flutter,
In there stepped a stately Raven of the saintly days of yore;
    Not the least obeisance made he; not a minute stopped or stayed he;
    But, with mien of lord or lady, perched above my chamber door—
Perched upon a bust of Pallas just above my chamber door—
        Perched, and sat, and nothing more.

Then this ebony bird beguiling my sad fancy into smiling,
By the grave and stern decorum of the countenance it wore,
"Though thy crest be shorn and shaven, thou," I said, "art sure no craven,
Ghastly grim and ancient Raven wandering from the Nightly shore—
Tell me what thy lordly name is on the Night's Plutonian shore!"
        Quoth the Raven "Nevermore."

    Much I marvelled this ungainly fowl to hear discourse so plainly,
Though its answer little meaning—little relevancy bore;
    For we cannot help agreeing that no living human being
    Ever yet was blessed with seeing bird above his chamber door—
Bird or beast upon the sculptured bust above his chamber door,
        With such name as "Nevermore."

    But the Raven, sitting lonely on the placid bust, spoke only
That one word, as if his soul in that one word he did outpour.
    Nothing farther then he uttered—not a feather then he fluttered—
    Till I scarcely more than muttered "Other friends have flown before—
On the morrow he will leave me, as my Hopes have flown before."
        Then the bird said "Nevermore."

    Startled at the stillness broken by reply so aptly spoken,
"Doubtless," said I, "what it utters is its only stock and store
    Caught from some unhappy master whom unmerciful Disaster
    Followed fast and followed faster till his songs one burden bore—
Till the dirges of his Hope that melancholy burden bore
        Of 'Never—nevermore'."

    But the Raven still beguiling all my fancy into smiling,
Straight I wheeled a cushioned seat in front of bird, and bust and door;
    Then, upon the velvet sinking, I betook myself to linking
    Fancy unto fancy, thinking what this ominous bird of yore—
What this grim, ungainly, ghastly, gaunt, and ominous bird of yore
        Meant in croaking "Nevermore."

This I sat engaged in guessing, but no syllable expressing
To the fowl whose fiery eyes now burned into my bosom's core;
    This and more I sat divining, with my head at ease reclining
    On the cushion's velvet lining that the lamp-light gloated o'er,
But whose velvet-violet lining with the lamp-light gloating o'er,
        She shall press, ah, nevermore!

Then, methought, the air grew denser, perfumed from an unseen censer
Swung by Seraphim whose foot-falls tinkled on the tufted floor.
    "Wretch," I cried, "thy God hath lent thee—by these angels he hath sent thee
    Respite—respite and nepenthe from thy memories of Lenore;
Quaff, oh quaff this kind nepenthe and forget this lost Lenore!"
        Quoth the Raven "Nevermore."

"Prophet!" said I, "thing of evil!—prophet still, if bird or devil!—
Whether Tempter sent, or whether tempest tossed thee here ashore,
    Desolate yet all undaunted, on this desert land enchanted—
    On this home by Horror haunted—tell me truly, I implore—
Is there—is there balm in Gilead?—tell me—tell me, I implore!"
        Quoth the Raven "Nevermore."

"Prophet!" said I, "thing of evil!—prophet still, if bird or devil!
By that Heaven that bends above us—by that God we both adore—
    Tell this soul with sorrow laden if, within the distant Aidenn,
    It shall clasp a sainted maiden whom the angels name Lenore—
Clasp a rare and radiant maiden whom the angels name Lenore."
        Quoth the Raven "Nevermore."

"Be that word our sign of parting, bird or fiend!" I shrieked, upstarting—
"Get thee back into the tempest and the Night's Plutonian shore!
    Leave no black plume as a token of that lie thy soul hath spoken!
    Leave my loneliness unbroken!—quit the bust above my door!
Take thy beak from out my heart, and take thy form from off my door!"
        Quoth the Raven "Nevermore."

And the Raven, never flitting, still is sitting, still is sitting
On the pallid bust of Pallas just above my chamber door;
   And his eyes have all the seeming of a demon's that is dreaming,
     And the lamp-light o'er him streaming throws his shadow on the floor;
And my soul from out that shadow that lies floating on the floor
        Shall be lifted—nevermore!

Martin Ontiveros

lives and works (and lurks) in the East Bay of Northern California.
He's never met a werewolf, vampire, or ghost he didn't like.